VMH
Vildi M. Hankes

The Adventures of Old Swifton Road

Lee's Incredible Journey

VMH Vikki M. Hankins™ Publishing
www.vmhpublishing.com

Manufactured in the United States of America

Hardback ISBN: 978-1-947928-05-3
Paperback ISBN: 978-1-947928-04-6

10 9 8 7 6 5 4 3 2 1

Book Cover Design: VMH Publishing
Illustrations: VMH Publishing
Cover Design Concept: William Christopher Scandrett
Illustrations Concept: William Christopher Scandrett

Publisher's Note:

This book is dedicated to my sweet Grandma Lee.

It was a bright Saturday morning
on Old Swifton Road.
Lee was in the living room reading
– doing what she was told.

Her mother said, "Go in there, so you won't bother me."
She knew all Lee would do is talk about Paleontology.

Lee loved fossils of animals and plants, but most of all dinosaurs. She begged to go to a museum to take some self-guided tours.

But her mother was often busy -
she ran a cattle farm.
And her phone rang so much; she
kept it strapped to her arm.

Lee kept herself busy learning
about old T-Rex bones.
On one particular morning, Lee
felt extra alone.

So she grabbed her backpack, her boots, and magnifying glass;
She took a rock-brush, a pencil, and her journal from class.

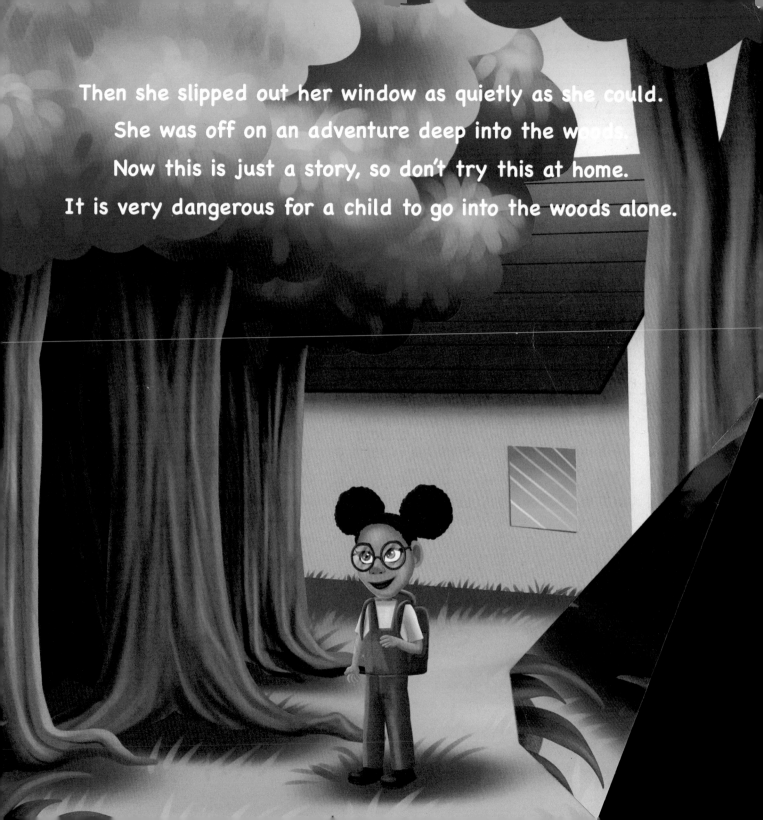

Then she slipped out her window as quietly as she could.
She was off on an adventure deep into the woods.
Now this is just a story, so don't try this at home.
It is very dangerous for a child to go into the woods alone.

Now Lee was ready for an adventure
with all of her gear.

And she made sure to step quietly, so
no animal would hear.

She searched and she searched for the perfect place to dig,

But then she heard some footsteps from something really big.

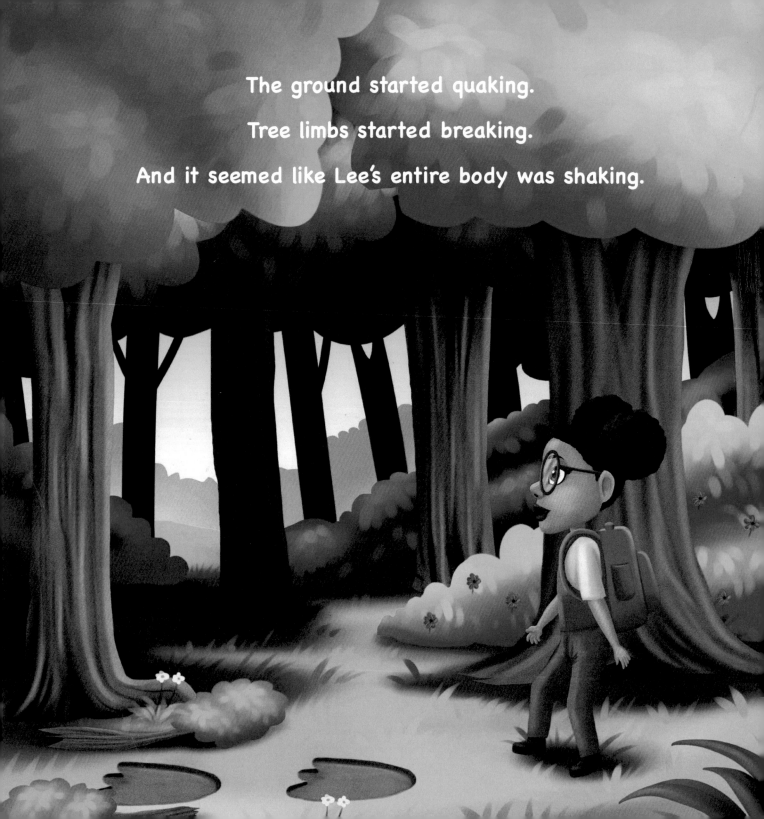

The ground started quaking.

Tree limbs started breaking.

And it seemed like Lee's entire body was shaking.

Now you'll never guess what exactly happened next.

Standing high above Lee was a Tyrannosaurus Rex!

Shaken and afraid, Lee quickly dried her tears,

Because she knew dinosaurs had been extinct for millions of years.

Lee gathered all her courage;

Well, as much as she could bring.

And she yelled so loud that she scared the poor thing.

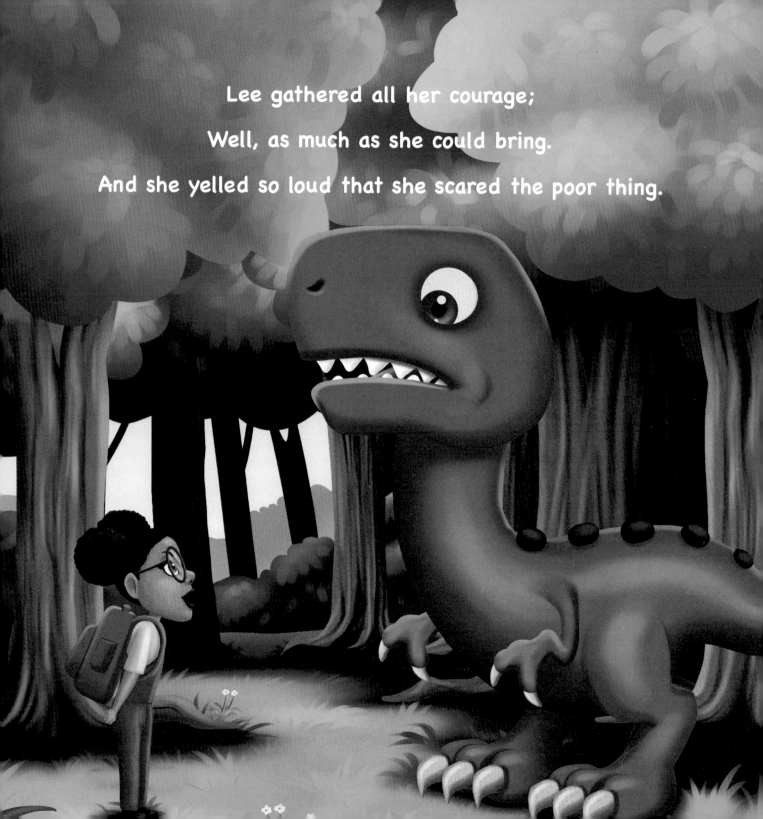

The T-Rex dropped to his knees and started to weep.

He seemed less like a predator and more like a sheep!

She rubbed his head as he started to purr,

But in the distance Lee could hear Mother calling for her.

She knew she had to get back home as quickly as possible. And no one would believe her – it just wasn't logical.

So she said "See you later!" to her newly found friend.

And she was more than confident that she would see him again.

By the time she got home, her mother was worried sick.

As soon as she saw Lee, she scooped her up quick.

She hugged her really tight and asked "Where have you been?"

Lee replied "Just playing with my imaginary friend."

Her mother said "Baby, don't scare me that way.

I'll make more time just for you, everyday."

So for an hour each day, they'd sit together and study.

And draw portraits of dinosaurs and make fossils with putty.

Now, If you ever hear a sound outside and you think it's a toad,

It might just be the dinosaur down on Old Swifton Road.

Vocabulary List for Lee's Incredible Journey

Paleontology: the branch of science concerned with fossil animals and plants

Fossils: any preserved remains, impression, or trace of any once-living thing

Museum: an institution that cares for a collection of artifacts and other objects of artistic, cultural, historical, or scientific importance

Cattle: a herd of cows

Magnifying Glass: a lens that is used to produce an enlarged image of an object

Rock-brush: a brush used to clean off fossils

Tyrannosaurus Rex: a large carnivorous dinosaur with sharp teeth and claw like front legs

Extinct: having no living members of a group or species

Weep: to cry

Predator: an animal that naturally preys on others

Logical: to make sense; reasonable

Confident: feeling sure or certain

Imaginary: pretend; not real

Portrait: a painting or picture

Putty: a material similar to clay or dough

Dinosaur Excavation Activity

Place some small dinosaur toys in an ice tray and freeze them.

Pour the ice cube "fossils" into a bucket.

Use warm water and a turkey baster to let your child thaw out their dinosaurs.

Write down each kind of dinosaur you discover.

Let your child draw a portrait of their favorite dinosaur!

Made in the USA
Columbia, SC
15 December 2018